W9-CHO-744

XANDER NASH:

SIBLING RIVALRY

WRITTEN BY HUNTER TALEN
ILLUSTRATED BY NEIL KLEID

Published by Creation By Design, LLC, Teaneck, NJ
www.creationbydesign.com

Text Copyright © 2010 by Creation By Design, LLC
Illustrations Copyright © 2010 by Creation By Design, LLC
All rights reserved. No part of this book may be reproduced in any form, except for brief quotations in reviews, without the written permission of the publisher.

Printed in: Canada
Cover & interior design: Creation By Design
Xander Nash and related characters by Creation By Design

ISBN: 978-0-9828077-5-0

Publisher's Cataloging-In-Publication Data
(Prepared by The Donohue Group, Inc.)

Talen, Hunter.
  Xander Nash. [2], Sibling rivalry / written by Hunter Talen ;
illustrated by Neil Kleid.

  p. : ill. ; cm.

  Includes index.
  ISBN: 978-0-9828077-5-0

  1. Bible stories, English--O.T.--Juvenile fiction. 2. Archaeology--
Juvenile fiction. 3. Time travel--Juvenile fiction. 4. Bible stories--
O.T.--Fiction. 5. Archaeology--Fiction. 6. Time travel--Fiction. 7.
Sibling rivalry--Fiction. 8. Adventure fiction. I. Kleid, Neil. II. Title.
III. Title: Sibling rivalry

PZ7.T3546 Xas 2010
[Fic]

Contents

Chapter 1

Something New

"Xander, close your eyes!"

Xander Nash lay on his bed, reading a book.

"Are they closed yet?" Kevin called from the hallway. "I'm coming into your room. Wait till you see what Mom and Dad just gave me!"

Xander was enjoying his book. He

didn't feel like being interrupted right now -- especially by his brother Kevin.

"Show me later," Xander said. "I'm busy now."

Xander kept on reading.

"C'mon, Xander!" Kevin cried. "Just close your eyes for one second. Then open them when I tell you to."

Xander could tell that Kevin wasn't going to leave him alone. "Fine," he sighed, shutting both his book and his eyes. "My eyes are closed."

Kevin stepped into the room. "Now open them," he said. "Tada!"

Xander opened his eyes. Kevin stood at the foot of his bed, wearing a colorful new sweater.

"Isn't it cool?" Kevin said. "It has so many different colors!"

Xander gazed at the sweater. "Yes, it's nice," he mumbled. Then he added, "Why did Mom and Dad give you a new sweater? It's not your birthday."

Kevin smiled. "I know," he replied. "Mom said she just saw it at the store and thought it would look great on me. And it does!"

Just then, Mom walked into Xander's bedroom.

"That sweater's perfect for you, Kevin," she said. She turned to Xander and asked, "Alexander, don't you agree?"

Mom and Dad were the only people in the world who called Xander by his full name instead of his nickname.

Xander didn't answer. Instead, he frowned.

"What bitter bug bit you this

morning?" Mom joked.

Xander didn't laugh. "Why did Kevin get a new sweater?" he grumbled. "It's not his birthday or anything."

"I think someone is jealous," Kevin teased.

"I'm not jealous," Xander insisted. "I just want to know why you got something new and I didn't."

Mom gently placed her arm on Xander's shoulder. "Now, Alexander dear, you're not behaving the way a nine-year-old brother should," she said softly. "Dad and I bought this sweater for Kevin because we thought it would look good on him. You know we don't always buy both of you gifts at the same time."

Xander was still frowning.

Kevin said, "Tell you what, Bro. Now that I have this new sweater, I'll give you my old blue one. It's still in good shape. And you're tall enough to wear it now."

A tear started to roll down Xander's cheek. "I don't want your hand-me-downs!" he cried. "I'm tired of always getting your hand-me-downs. It's not fair!"

Xander's sudden outburst surprised Mom. She tried to hug him, but Xander pulled away.

"I'm going outdoors," Xander announced, wiping his cheek. "I feel like exploring."

Xander's favorite activity -- besides reading books -- was exploring the neighborhood. It was always exciting for him. He never knew what he might find hidden behind a tree or around the bend.

Xander put on his favorite brown fedora hat. It made him feel like a real explorer.

Next, he put on his explorer's belt. It had pockets that held all his exploring equipment--a flashlight, a compass, a water canteen, and a writing pad.

The pockets also held two maps -- a neighborhood map and a map of the world. After all, Xander never knew where his adventures might take him.

Just as Xander was about to leave the house, Mom said, "Since you're going out, dear, why don't you take Mitts with you? He needs to be walked now."

Xander smiled. He was always happy to walk his dog. Mitts was the world's best dog. Xander had named him Mitts because each of the pug's large paws reminded him of a baseball catcher's mitt.

"Here, Mitts," Xander called. The pug came running right away.

"Good dog," Xander said, leaning down to rub Mitts' wrinkly face and curly tail. "At least *you* don't give me your hand-me-downs," he joked.

Xander fastened the leash on Mitts and led him outdoors. The dog barked happily, jumping up and down.

The two strolled along the sidewalk. Soon they had gone several blocks.

"Mitts, I have an idea," Xander said. "Let's explore in the park across the street."

Xander and Mitts crossed at the corner and walked into the park. No one else was around.

Just then, Xander looked above the trees. He couldn't believe his eyes!

"Look, Mitts!" he cried. "Look at that huge rainbow in the sky! I didn't even notice it before!"

Xander walked closer. He saw that one end of the rainbow touched down right in the middle of the park!

Xander moved slowly toward the rainbow. Suddenly, Mitts broke away from Xander and raced ahead.

"Mitts, come back!" Xander called.

The curious pug kept on running. He was attracted to the many colors of the rainbow. He ran until he reached the spot where the rainbow touched the ground.

What happened next really shocked Xander. Mitts leapt onto the rainbow--as if he were jumping onto a playground slide! Xander raced toward him as fast as he could.

Xander reached the bottom of the rainbow, but he couldn't stop Mitts. The dog was now running up along the arc.

"Mitts, get down from there right now!" Xander cried. "You'll fall off and hurt yourself!"

Mitts kept running along the rainbow. Xander needed to rescue him. He had no choice but to follow the dog.

Xander expected the rainbow to be slippery; well, really he expected to not be able to touch it at all. The rainbow felt cool to the touch and not smooth; it felt more like carpeting. When he moved his hand away, some of the color came with it, like flecks of glitter.

Xander stepped onto the rainbow and began to crawl toward Mitts. He struggled to keep his balance on the curve.

In a span of several minutes, Xander crawled steadily. Yet Mitts stayed far ahead of him.

For the first time, Xander looked down. He was high off the ground!

Suddenly, Xander realized that he was no longer crawling. Instead, a strange force -- like a magnet -- was pulling him along the colorful arc. He moved up along the rainbow, as if on a conveyor belt -- without even trying! Ahead of him, Mitts was moving up, too.

Where in the world were the two of them headed?

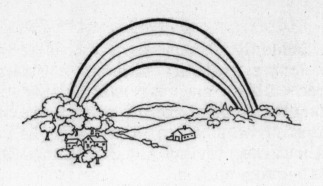

Chapter 2

A Scary Ride

Xander and Mitts continued to move up along the giant rainbow. It felt like the start of a roller-coaster ride. The two rose higher and higher at a steady pace.

Soon, Xander reached the very top of the arc. It was there that he finally caught up with Mitts.

Neither Xander nor Mitts were now moving. Both of them had stopped at the top of the rainbow.

Xander grabbed his dog and held him tightly. "Oh, Mitts!" he cried. "Look at the mess you got us into! We're stuck on this rainbow, and I have no idea how to get down!"

Mitts whimpered, as if to say, "I'm sorry."

Xander looked down from the top of the arc. He was scared. He and Mitts were so high off the ground that they could no longer see anyone on Earth. All Xander saw were puffs of white floating in the sky.

"Mitts!" Xander gasped. "We're above the clouds!"

The two of them sat still at the top of the rainbow. Time passed slowly. Xander thought about Mom and Dad and Kevin. They would surely be worried about him-- if only they knew where he was!

Xander wondered if he and Mitts

could climb down the rainbow. Maybe it would be like climbing down a ladder. Maybe not.

Xander was about to test his idea when suddenly he began to move forward along the rainbow. He held on tightly to Mitts, who sat on his lap.

"Hold on, Mitts!" Xander cried. "We're sliding down the rain-BOOOOOOOOOOWWWWWWWW!"

Xander and Mitts zoomed rapidly down the steep arc. Soon, they saw no more white clouds. Instead, a blur of bright colors flashed across their eyes. Red! Orange! Yellow! Green! Blue! Purple!

Xander kept a tight grip on Mitts. After several minutes, the two of them came to a sudden stop.

Xander looked around. He realized that he and Mitts were back on the ground. Yet they weren't in the park.

Instead, they stood in a large, open field.

"Mitts, I have no idea where we are," Xander said.

"I know where you are," a voice behind them said.

Xander turned around quickly. A young man who looked about seventeen years old stood facing him. He wore a coat of many bright colors. The colors seemed to be connected to the end of the rainbow.

"Who...who are you?" Xander asked, holding Mitts tightly.

"My name is Joseph," the man replied. "And who are you?"

Xander put out his hand to shake with Joseph. "I am Xander Nash," he said, "and this is my dog, Mitts."

Xander gazed at Joseph's colorful coat.

It seemed familiar to him, but he wasn't sure why.

Then, suddenly, it all came back to Xander.

"Are we in... the land of Canaan?" he asked, gasping.

"Yes," Joseph said, laughing. "Where else could we be?"

"Then you really *are* Joseph!" Xander cried. "You're wearing the colored coat your father Jacob gave you as a gift."

Joseph smiled. "That is correct," he said. "But how do you know about my coat? Do you live near my family in Canaan? Do you know my eleven brothers?"

"No," Xander replied, shaking his head. "I don't know them personally. I only know about you because you're in the Bible. I don't live here. I come from the future."

Joseph looked puzzled. Xander guessed that he didn't know what the future was. He would not even know what the Bible was!

"I traveled back in time," Xander explained. "I rode on a rainbow. And I think it was your coat that created the rainbow!" Xander decided not to talk about the Bible again to Joseph, as every movie about time travel that Xander saw warned about people in the past learning too much about their future.

Joseph shook his head. "No, Xander," he said. "God is the Creator of all things. It is God who created the rainbow, just as He first created it back in the days of Noah. For some reason, God wanted you to travel to Canaan to meet me. Maybe we share something in common."

Xander thought for a moment. He remembered the colored sweater that

Mom and Dad had given Kevin.

"We *do* share something in common!" he exclaimed. "Your father gave you a colorful coat that made your brothers jealous, right?"

Joseph nodded.

"And my parents gave my brother Kevin a colorful sweater that made *me* jealous," Xander explained.

"Well," Joseph said, placing a hand on Xander's shoulder, "I hope the colored sweater didn't make you want to hurt your brother. Unfortunately, that's how my coat has affected my brothers."

Xander's eyes grew large. "You mean your brothers want to hurt you?" he gasped. "Just because of a coat?"

"I'm afraid so," Joseph sighed. "They grew very jealous over a gift that I never even asked for."

At that moment, Xander realized that Kevin had never asked Mom and Dad for his gift either.

"And I never should have told my family about my two dreams," Joseph continued. "That only made things worse."

"What dreams?" Xander asked.

"In my first dream," Joseph began, "my brothers and I were bundling grain in a field. Their eleven bundles bowed down to my bundle. My brothers assumed I was telling them what I thought the dream meant -- that I will rule over them some day. That was a big mistake. They didn't like the whole idea, especially since all my brothers but one are older than I am."

Joseph continued, "I wasn't trying to say that I was better than they are. I was just telling them my dream. They are my family and I wanted to share it with them. Maybe I should have kept them to myself."

"What was your second dream?" Xander asked.

"In my second dream, the sun and moon and eleven stars bowed down to me," Joseph explained. "My father, Jacob believed the sun was a symbol for him, and the moon was a symbol for my mother."

"And the eleven stars were symbols for your brothers?" Xander asked.

"Exactly," Joseph sighed. "As before, my brothers believed that the dream meant that I would rule over my family one day. I cannot control the dreams God sends me. You can imagine how angry that made them."

Xander thought for a while. Then he asked, "Where are you headed now?"

Joseph said, "My brothers are in the field, feeding our family's flock of sheep. My father asked me to see how they are doing, and I always do what my father asks of me. But I'm afraid."

"Afraid of what?" Xander asked.

"Afraid of what they may do to me," Joseph replied.

Joseph pointed in the distance. He said, "Those are my brothers up ahead. They see me coming. They have angry looks on their faces. I fear they may be planning to kill me."

Now Xander felt afraid, too. "Should I stay behind?" he asked.

"No, I don't believe they would hurt you. They have nothing against you, and they are not bad people," Joseph replied. "Come with me. Perhaps you will be able to help me."

Xander doubted that he could help Joseph. But he didn't want to leave him alone with his brothers.

Xander walked with Joseph. He hoped the brothers wouldn't harm them. But who knew what dangers might lay ahead?

Chapter 3

Evil Doings

Xander and Joseph approached the brothers.

"Well, look who's here," sneered Reuben, the oldest brother. "It's our very special brother, Joseph."

"To what do we owe this great honor?" added Simeon.

"Have you come to tell us another of

your dreams, and how you will rule over us?" Levi said angrily.

"No, no, no," Joseph replied. "I come in peace. Father asked me to check on you."

"Oh, Father," Judah mocked.

"You mean Father who chose you as his favorite son?" said Issachar.

"And Father who gave you a special colored coat?" added Zebulon.

"Unlike the *plain* coats that we must wear!" sneered Dan.

One brother, Naftali, stared at Xander. "Who's your little friend, Joseph?" he asked. "Is he someone else who will rule over us, too?"

Xander felt his heart beating faster. He was very afraid.

"Hi, I'm Xand--" he began.

"Quiet!" Gad shouted. "Speak only when you are spoken to, boy! We asked our question to Joseph, not to you."

Joseph pointed to Xander. "This is Xander," he explained, "and we just met."

"And where are you from, boy?" Asher barked.

Xander shook in fear. He was too scared to speak.

"Answer the question, boy!" Asher commanded.

Xander took a deep breath. "I'm--I'm Xander Nash," he said softly.

"Speak up, boy!" Simeon demanded. "I can barely hear you."

Xander took another deep breath. "I am Xander Nash," he repeated louder.

"This is my dog Mitts. We come from the future."

The eleven brothers looked puzzled. "What do you mean?" asked Reuben.

"My dog Mitts and I traveled back in time," Xander explained. "We come from a time thousands of years from now."

Levi wagged a finger angrily at Xander. "I do not believe you," he declared. "Prove to us that you are from the future." Mitts snarled at the brothers, and moved between them and Xander.

Xander tried to think of a way to prove that he was telling the truth. Suddenly, he had an idea. He removed the flashlight from his explorer's belt.

"This is a flashlight," Xander said to the brothers. He turned the light on and off for them to see. "You've never seen one, because it won't be invented for thousands of years."

The brothers watched curiously as the light appeared and disappeared.

"It could be a trick of the sun," Judah sneered. "I still don't believe that you are from the future."

Xander had another idea. He showed the brothers his compass. "This is a compass," he explained. "It tells you the direction you are facing. Since I am facing the morning sun, the compass tells me that direction is east. That's because the sun rises in the east."

The brothers leaned in closer to watch the compass work.

"That's nothing special," Issachar growled. "The sun is merely making the needle point that way."

"No," Xander objected. "The sun isn't pulling the needle. It's a magnetic field that's pulling it."

The brothers looked even more confused and angry.

Suddenly, Zebulon grabbed Xander. "This boy is a spy!" he cried. "He came with Joseph to spy on us!"

"I am *not* a spy!" Xander protested. "I just got here." Mitts grabbed Zebulon's coat in his teeth, trying to pull. Unfortunately, Mitts was too small to have much of an effect.

Gad grabbed Joseph. Then Asher tried to grab Mitts, but the dog began to run quickly.

"That's right, Mitts!" Xander cried. "Run fast! Don't let these bad men catch you!"

Mitts kept on running. The brothers chased after him.

The dog reached the spot where the

sheep were grazing. The sheep became scared and began to run, too.

It was a wild scene! The sheep were running in all directions!

The brothers had to stop chasing Mitts in order to gather their sheep. After a while, they had the animals together again.

Xander was worried because he didn't see Mitts. "Where is he?" he wondered aloud.

The brothers walked across the field. After a while, Naftali called, "I found the dog!"

Everyone walked to Naftali, who stood near a pit.

"The dog has fallen into this pit," Naftali laughed. "It serves the animal right for causing all this trouble."

Xander looked down into the pit. Mitts was barking loudly. Xander was glad that he did not seem to be hurt at all from the fall.

"I have an idea," Zebulon announced. "Let's kill Joseph and his spy friend Xander. Then we'll throw their bodies into this pit. We'll tell Father that Joseph was killed by a wild animal. We can even say it was this wild, angry dog!"

"We can tear the colored coat and show it to Father as proof of the attack," Naftali added.

The other brothers liked the idea. Only one brother, Reuben, objected to the plan.

"Brothers, there's no need for us to commit murder," Reuben said. "I have a better idea. Let's simply leave Joseph and Xander in the pit. They'll be trapped there. Sooner or later, they really *will* be killed by an animal that passes by. And we won't have blood on our hands."

The brothers liked Reuben's idea. What the brothers didn't know was that Reuben was feeling bad about harming Joseph. He knew that the other brothers were just angry, and that if they really hurt Joseph, they would regret it later.

Reuben planned to come back that night and free Joseph and Xander, after the brothers had calmed down.

With great force, they threw Joseph and Xander into the deep pit to join Mitts. Joseph and Xander got up and shook the dust off, bruised but alive.

Joseph's brothers then walked away from the pit, laughing at their evil deed.

However, there was one thing the brothers didn't know. Reuben alone was secretly thinking that he didn't want his brother to die -- no matter how it might happen. He planned to come back later

and rescue Joseph, and Xander, as well.

Joseph, Xander, and Mitts were now helpless in the dirty pit. Xander feared that a wild, hungry animal might find them soon.

Could Reuben -- or anyone else -- save them in time?

Chapter 4

A Change of Plan

Joseph stood at the bottom of the deep pit. He scooped out dirt in several places along the walls.

"What are you doing?" Xander asked.

"I'm seeing how strong these dirt walls are," Joseph explained. "If they are strong enough, we can dig steps and climb out of the pit."

Xander imagined that Joseph was as

scared as he was, but he certainly didn't show it. Even at only seventeen years old, Joseph seemed so calm, like he knew everything would work out all right. Kevin was already thirteen, and Xander was sure he would be crying and screaming if he was thrown into a pit.

Xander watched as Joseph continued to scrape at the walls, trying to form steps. He climbed a few steps but fell back to the bottom of the pit.

"I think the walls are too steep to climb," Xander said.

Suddenly, Mitts began to bark loudly. Xander saw what was upsetting him. A small black spider was crawling on one of the dog's paws. Xander quickly brushed away the spider and stepped on it.

"Quiet, Mitts," Xander said, petting him. "That spider won't bother you anymore."

Joseph looked at Xander. "It may be better to let the dog bark," Joseph said. "It will draw the attention of anyone walking nearby. They will see that we are trapped here in the pit."

"Okay, Mitts, bark all you like," Xander said. But now the dog remained quiet.

Meanwhile, Joseph's brothers were not far from the pit, eating and laughing. Only Reuben had left the group to watch the sheep in the field.

Suddenly, the brothers saw travelers approaching in the distance.

"Look!" cried Simeon. "It's a band of merchants. I wonder what they are selling."

"Or buying," Judah added, snapping his fingers as if he had an idea.

"What do you mean?" the brothers

asked.

"Why should we leave Joseph in the pit to die?" Judah explained. "We could sell him as a slave to the merchants. That way we will make some money, and Joseph will still be out of our lives for good. Besides, for someone who thinks he will be king over us, working as a slave will teach him a lesson."

The brothers liked Judah's idea. Patting each other on the back, they agreed to sell Joseph.

Soon the merchants came by. They were Ishmaelites on their way to Egypt. The brothers signaled them to stop.

"Would you like to buy a young, strong slave?" Judah asked the Ishmaelite leader.

"Where is he?" the leader asked.

"Come with us," Judah replied.

Together, the brothers and the travelers walked to the edge of the pit. Joseph, Xander, and Mitts stood at the bottom.

The brothers threw down two ropes. "Grab onto the ropes and we'll pull you out of the pit," Levi yelled.

"We're being rescued!" Joseph cried to Xander. "I believe God has answered our prayers."

Joseph grabbed the end of one rope. Xander held Mitts and grabbed the end of the other rope. "Stay with me," Xander told his dog.

The brothers tugged hard and steadily on each rope. Slowly, the captives were lifted out of the pit. At last they were on the ground.

Joseph brushed off his colored coat. "Thank you. Finally, you have come to your senses and set us free," he said to his brothers.

"Hardly!" Judah laughed. He turned to the Ishmaelite leader and asked, "How much will you pay for these fine slaves?"

Xander gulped loudly. "Sl-slaves?" he cried. Xander had learned all about slavery in school. It was clearly wrong to own another person, but this many years ago, in this place, it happened all the time.

The Ishmaelite leader looked closely at Joseph and Xander. He studied Mitts, too.

"I will give you twenty pieces of silver for the three," the leader announced.

"It's a deal," Judah said. He shook hands with the buyer and accepted the coins.

Before handing over the slaves,

Naftali pulled off Joseph's colored coat. "We'll need this," he reminded his brothers.

The Ishmaelites took Joseph, Xander, and Mitts and continued on their way to Egypt.

The brothers went to the field to gather their sheep.

Meanwhile, Reuben returned from the field. He planned to secretly rescue Joseph now. He looked into the pit. To his great surprise, it was empty!

"Oh, no!" Reuben cried. "Joseph must have been killed and eaten by a wild animal!"

Reuben caught up with his brothers in the field. They told him that they had sold Joseph as a slave.

"Oh, no!" Reuben wailed. "Since I am the oldest brother, Father will surely blame me for this!"

"No," Gad said. "We will trick Father into thinking that a wild animal really ate Joseph."

The brothers had eaten a goat for dinner, and from preparing it there was a large puddle of blood. They took turns dipping Joseph's coat into the goat's blood.

"This blood looks like human blood," Gad said. "We'll show Father the bloody coat. He'll think it is Joseph's blood. He'll think Joseph was killed by an animal."

Reuben agreed to the plan. He had planned to save Joseph, but now it was too late to do anything. The brothers laughed as they made their way home. They thought they were now rid of Joseph for good. Or were they?

Chapter 5

Rising and Falling

Joseph and Xander traveled with the Ishmaelites toward Egypt. Mitts sat on Xander's lap.

Xander couldn't believe that he had been sold as a slave. He knew that slavery was against the law in modern times. But, of course, he wasn't in modern times right now.

What Xander didn't know was that big surprises were about to happen. Xander tried to remember the Bible story about what happened to Joseph, but he couldn't recall all of the details. There was nothing he could do but sit back and wait to see what would happen.

The Ishmaelite merchants did not hold on to their captives for long. When they arrived in Egypt, they sold the slaves to a rich man named Potiphar. He was an officer of Egypt's chief ruler, Pharaoh.

Xander's eyes widened when he saw Potiphar's home. "This looks like a king's palace!" he exclaimed.

Even Mitts barked when he saw the huge house.

Potiphar turned to Joseph. "Yes, I have a large home," he announced. "And you are now my servants. You will have many duties to perform."

Potiphar described their jobs. "Each day, you will wash the walls and floors of my home. You will do the laundry. You will prepare the meals for me, my wife Zuleika and our children. Is that clear?"

Xander realized that Mom did those same jobs every day in their home. He wondered if she ever felt like a slave. When, and if, he ever got home, he would make sure she knew how he appreciated everything she did for him and Mitts.

Joseph bowed to Potiphar with respect. "Whatever you say, we are glad to do for you, Master," Joseph said.

Potiphar smiled. He liked the positive attitude of this new slave.

Day after day, Joseph and Xander worked hard. They were kept busy from the moment they woke in the morning until they fell exhausted into their beds at night. Xander made sure that Mitts always stayed by his side and caused no trouble in the house.

Xander never worked so hard in his life - cooking, cleaning, laundry - he was too tired to even miss his family. Well, almost.

Joseph did his job so well that, in time, Potiphar rewarded him with a promotion. Joseph was put in charge of Potiphar's entire household. He made sure that all the other servants in the home did their jobs properly.

Joseph felt bad that Xander was in this situation because of him, and he did everything in his power to make this life easier on Xander and Mitts.

Over the days and weeks, Xander noticed something. Everyone around him was changing , getting older, moving through life. Joseph had needed to shave a few times. But no changes were happening to Xander and Mitts. They weren't getting any older. He could tell since he didn't need a haircut or cut his finger nails. It was a weird feeling.

One morning, Joseph and Xander were walking through the house, checking that all was okay. Xander noticed someone peeking at them from behind a curtain.

At first, Xander couldn't tell who the person was. Then he stared hard. It was Zuleika, Potiphar's wife.

Xander started to walk toward her. Joseph grabbed his arm.

"Don't go near her," Joseph ordered. "Stay right here."

"Why?" Xander asked. "Potiphar's wife may need something."

Joseph shook his head. "No, Xander," he said firmly. "Zuleika is just making trouble. For several weeks now, she has tried to kiss me and get me to sneak around with her. I've told her no every time, but she keeps on trying."

"Why don't you tell Potiphar?" Xander asked.

"It's not that simple," Joseph explained. "Even though I am head of all the servants, I am still just a servant. If I tell Potiphar what his wife is doing, he may not believe me. He may punish me instead of her."

"That's not fair," Xander said.

"You're right, Xander," Joseph replied. "But as you can see, life does not always seem fair. We can only pray to God for His help."

For many days, Xander thought about Joseph's words. Would Potiphar really punish Joseph, even if Joseph were telling the truth?

Before long, Xander had the answer.

One day, he and Joseph heard someone screaming in the house. All the servants ran to see who it was. It was Zuleika.

Suddenly, Zuleika came into the room. Potiphar stood next to her. She angrily pointed a finger at Joseph.

"Joseph attacked me and tried to kiss me!" she screamed to her husband. "He dragged me into our bedroom!" Potiphar's wife was holding a piece of Joseph's shirt in her hand.

Xander's heart was racing fast.

Potiphar's face turned red with anger. He looked at Joseph. He could see that Joseph's shirt had been ripped.

"Is this true, Joseph?" he asked sharply.

Joseph bowed with respect. "No,

Master, it is not true. I was never in your wife's bedroom. I did not attack her, she tried to pull me in, and tore my shirt."

Zuleika screamed, "Animal!! You did do it! And now you try to blame me?"

Potiphar looked angrily at Joseph. "Are you calling my wife a liar?" he demanded.

Joseph knew there was no answer that would satisfy Potiphar. He bowed his head and said, "I place my fate in God's hands, Master."

Potiphar cried, "Guards! Seize Joseph! Throw him into prison immediately!

Two guards grabbed Joseph by the arms.

Xander jumped forward to defend his friend. "No, Master. Joseph is telling the truth. He would never do anything against you or Mrs. Potiphar." Xander pleaded. "You have to believe him!"

But Xander's words fell on deaf ears. In fact, Xander's speaking out of turn seemed to anger Potiphar even more.

A third guard asked, "Master, what about his friend Xander? Shall we take him as well?"

"Yes!" Potiphar commanded. "And the little dog, too! Place them all into a prison cell right now!"

Xander grabbed Mitts and tried to run away. However, a ring of guards quickly surrounded them.

Within minutes, Joseph and Xander found themselves in a dark prison cell. The floor was cold and damp. Xander held Mitts tightly as he shook with fear.

"Oh, Joseph!" Xander cried. "Whatever are we going to do now?"

"Pray to God," Joseph said, standing straight. "That is our only hope."

Chapter 6

Strange Dreams

Xander couldn't believe how quickly everything had gone from good to bad. Just minutes ago, Joseph had been the head of Potiphar's servants. Now he and Xander and Mitts were locked up in prison!

Suddenly they heard a man's voice in the dark. "Welcome to this nightmare," the stranger said.

Xander held Mitts tightly as he tried to make out the figure that sat in front of him.

"Who...who are you?" Xander asked, his voice trembling.

"I am Pharaoh's chief baker," the man replied. "Or, rather I should say, *was* Pharaoh's chief baker."

"I am Xander Nash," Xander said. "Why are you in prison?"

The baker replied, "Pharaoh thought we were poisoning his food."

"Who is 'we'?" Xander asked curiously.

"The chief butler and myself," the baker explained. "Of course, we were not poisoning our master. It was a lie that landed us in this prison."

"We are also here because of a lie," Xander said.

For a minute, all was quiet. Then the baker said, "I fear something bad is about to happen. For last night, the butler and I each dreamed a strange dream."

Suddenly, the butler spoke up, for he was also in the dark cell. "I was Pharaoh's chief butler," he said. "And neither the chief baker nor I know what our dreams mean."

Joseph sat up. "Dreams?" he asked. "Please, each of you describe your dream to me. With God's help, I will tell you what it means."

"Who are you?" the butler asked.

"I am Joseph," Joseph replied. "Like you, I was thrown into prison because of a lie. Please, tell me your dream."

"Joseph is really good at interpreting dreams," Xander added, although he had his doubts if this was a good idea. He remembered the brothers' reaction to Joseph interpreting dreams.

The butler took a deep breath. "In my dream, I saw a grapevine with three branches," he began. "Ripe grapes grew on the branches. I squeezed the grapes into Pharaoh's cup. Then I handed the cup to Pharaoh."

Joseph thought for a moment. Then he said, "The three branches mean three days. In three days from now, Pharaoh will give you back your old job. You will be serving wine to your master again, as you once did."

"Hooray!" the butler cried. "Thank you, Joseph. You have given me hope for the future."

Joseph replied, "Please remember me once you are freed from prison. Please tell Pharaoh how I was able to interpret your dream, so that Pharaoh might free me as well."

Now, the chief baker was eager to tell Joseph his dream.

"In my dream," he began, "I had three baskets of bread on my head. The basket on top held many different kinds of bread for Pharaoh. Suddenly, birds flew down and ate those breads."

Again, Joseph thought for a moment. Then he said, "The three baskets mean three days. In three days, Pharaoh will order you to be hanged from a tree. The birds will then peck at you."

"Ew, gross!" Xander cried.

The baker was very upset. He hoped that Joseph was wrong about the meaning of his dream.

Three days later, Joseph was proven right. Pharaoh freed the chief butler from prison and gave him back his old job.

Yet the chief baker was not as lucky. Pharaoh had him hanged from a tree, just as Joseph had predicted.

Xander felt sad, yet he was also hopeful. "Joseph," he said, "soon the chief butler will tell Pharaoh about your special talent. Then, we will be let out of prison, too!"

"We'll see," Joseph replied. "We'll see."

Unfortunately, things did not work out as Xander had hoped. After the butler was freed from prison, he forgot all about Joseph.

Joseph, Xander, and Mitts were still locked in prison. Would they ever get out now?

Chapter 7

A Lucky Break

Joseph, Xander, and Mitts remained in prison... for two years! It only felt like a couple of days to Xander, but he could see the toll it was having on Joseph. Clearly, God was making it seem so short a time for Xander to protect him.

During that time, Xander thought about his family often. He missed Mom and Dad a lot. He even missed Kevin. He knew they missed him as well. He wished he could go back and be with all of them again. But how?

Every day, Xander grew sadder and sadder. And every day, he and Joseph prayed to God for help.

Finally, the two of them got a lucky break.

One night, Pharaoh had two strange dreams. None of his advisors or magicians could tell him what the dreams meant.

At last, the chief butler remembered Joseph's special talent, and told Pharaoh about it.

Pharaoh immediately sent for Joseph. Xander and Mitts were allowed to come with him. Before they could see the Pharaoh they were given a bath and fancy new clothes. Xander insisted on keeping his Fedora tight on his head.

Xander stepped into Pharaoh's palace and gazed in amazement. "Wow!" he whispered to Mitts. "I thought Potiphar's home was fancy. But this place is *really* unbelievable!"

Pharaoh faced Joseph and said, "I have been told that you are able to understand the meaning of dreams."

Joseph bowed his head in respect. "It is not I who interprets dreams, Your Highness," he replied. "It is God. He allows me to understand their meaning."

Pharaoh was satisfied with Joseph's answer.

"I had two strange dreams recently," Pharaoh continued. "In the first, I saw seven fat, healthy cows come out of the Nile River. They ate grass along the riverbank. Then, seven skinny cows came out of the Nile and swallowed the seven fat cows. Yet the skinny cows remained skinny!"

"That is unusual," Joseph remarked.

"And what was your second dream, Your Highness?"

Pharaoh said, "In my second dream, I saw seven fat, healthy stalks of grain. Then I saw seven other stalks of grain that were thin and dried up. The thin stalks swallowed the fat stalks until there was nothing left. Yet the thin stalks of grain remained thin!"

Joseph thought carefully. Then he spoke.

"Your two dreams carry the same message," he explained. "The seven fat cows and the seven healthy grain stalks mean seven good years of farming and food production in Egypt."

Pharaoh looked pleased.

Joseph continued. "However," he cautioned, "the seven skinny cows and the seven thin grain stalks mean seven years of famine and starvation in Egypt

that will follow the seven good years. The seven years of hunger will be so bad that people everywhere will forget the seven good years."

Now Pharaoh did not look pleased at all.

"Tell me, Joseph," he asked, "why did I have two dreams with the same message? Why not just one dream?"

Joseph explained, "The two dreams indicate that the seven good years will start immediately."

Pharaoh was satisfied with Joseph's answer.

"Joseph," Pharaoh said, "since you alone seem to understand what is about to happen, what would you suggest that I do?"

Xander listened carefully, since he was curious how Joseph would answer.

Joseph said, "Your Highness, I advise you to choose a wise person to rule under you as second-in-command in Egypt. This person will make sure that during the seven good years, enough food is set aside and stored safely until it is needed during the seven years of hunger."

Pharaoh smiled. "And who shall this wise person be?" he asked.

Joseph remained silent, with his head bowed. Xander stood quietly behind him.

"Choose Joseph," Xander mouthed silently to Pharaoh, while pointing to his friend. "Choose Joseph!"

"I have made my choice," Pharaoh announced. "Joseph, you shall be my second-in-command for the coming fourteen years. You shall be in charge of collecting and giving out all food in the land of Egypt."

Pharaoh placed his own ring on Joseph's finger as a sign of Joseph's new job and power. He gave Joseph fancy clothes to wear, plus a gold necklace. Xander preferred his own clothes, and when they were returned to him they had been washed and pressed for him to wear.

In addition, he gave Joseph a royal chariot for riding around the vast land of Egypt.

Xander was happy for Joseph. He ran over and hugged him.

"God has really answered our prayers!" Xander cried. "You're Egypt's vice-president now!"

But deep down, Xander was also worried. Would he and Mitts be stuck in Egypt, away from his own family, forever?

Chapter 8

Food and Family

Although it only seemed like a few days to Xander, the next seven years went exactly as Joseph had predicted.

For seven years, all the farmers in Egypt grew plenty of crops. There was more than enough food for every family and person in the land.

During that time, Joseph kept very busy. He made sure that all the extra grain that grew was stored away safely in storehouses.

Xander also stayed quite busy. He worked as Joseph's assistant. He traveled with Joseph from city to city across the vast land of Egypt. They rode in Joseph's royal chariot. Even Mitts got to ride, too!

As the years passed for everyone but Xander and Mitts, Joseph's face changed. He looked more like a grown man, not like the teenager he had once been.

Xander did not age at all during his time in Egypt. The reason was simple. Because he had traveled back in time, he remained a nine-year-old -- just as he was when he left home.

During the time of plenty, Joseph and Xander made sure that all extra grain was set aside in storehouses. Not a kernel of grain was wasted.

Then, once it was over, everything changed. Just as Joseph had predicted, the crops in Egypt stopped growing.

Across the land, not one person had food to eat.

"Open the storehouses!" Joseph commanded.

"Give out the stored grain!" Xander shouted.

"Ruff, ruff!" Mitts barked.

Across the land, workers handed out bags of grain to the hungry Egyptians. Thanks to Joseph's careful planning, every Egyptian now had enough food to eat.

The shortage of food was not in Egypt alone. There was no food in neighboring lands as well. People from those places had to travel to Egypt to buy food for their families.

In Canaan, Jacob's family was starving.

"Go to Egypt and bring back food," Jacob ordered his sons.

"Shall we all go?" Reuben asked.

"No," replied Jacob. "Benjamin will stay at home with me. He is the youngest. He will be safe here."

Jacob's ten sons made the long journey to Egypt. When they arrived, they went straight to the storehouse where food was being given out.

Joseph was working at the storehouse. Xander was there, too. Xander couldn't believe it when he saw the ten men approaching.

"Joseph, look!" he cried. "It's your broth--"

Joseph quickly covered Xander's mouth. "Shhh!" Joseph whispered. "I recognize my brothers. Yet they will not know me, since I now look different than when they last saw me."

"But why don't you tell them who you are?" Xander asked softly. "You're second-in-command to Pharaoh. You don't need to be afraid of your brothers anymore."

Joseph smiled. "I know," he nodded. "But I have my reasons. You will understand everything very soon. Be patient, Xander."

Then Joseph added, "Xander, hide now, so my brothers do not see you. Since you have not aged, they will surely recognize you. And they will recognize Mitts, too."

Xander and Mitts quickly hid behind the door of the storehouse.

Soon, the brothers reached the front of the food line. Just as Joseph had expected, they didn't recognize their own brother!

"Who are you, and where are you

from?" Joseph asked them.

"We are brothers from Canaan," Reuben said. "We have come to buy food for our family back home."

Joseph looked angry. "No, you are spies!" he growled. "You will be thrown into prison!"

"No, please!" Reuben begged. "We are not spies. We are only ten brothers here for food. Another brother disappeared many years ago, and our youngest brother is at home with our father."

Joseph gave a doubtful look. "If you are telling the truth, then prove it," he ordered. "Return home with food, and then come back here with your youngest brother. Then I will know you are not spies."

Joseph allowed all the brothers but one to leave Egypt. He forced Simeon to stay behind. "I will free him after you return with your youngest brother," Joseph declared.

Xander was still hiding behind the storehouse door. He couldn't believe how cruelly Joseph had treated his brothers. Joseph had promised to explain his actions soon, but Xander could hardly wait!

Meanwhile, the nine brothers journeyed back to Canaan with food for the family. They told their father all that had happened in Egypt.

Jacob still refused to let Benjamin travel to Egypt. "I fear something bad will happen to him," Jacob declared.

Over time, Jacob's family ran out of the food that had been brought from Egypt. The brothers knew they couldn't return to Egypt for more food if Benjamin wasn't with them. They also knew Simeon would remain a prisoner until Benjamin returned with them.

"Please, Father," Judah begged Jacob. "I will be personally responsible for Benjamin's safety in Egypt."

Jacob shook his head. "Okay, take Benjamin with you," he said, his voice trembling. "I just pray to God that I will not regret my decision later."

The ten brothers journeyed back to Egypt. They were relieved to find that Simeon was okay. All eleven brothers bowed respectfully to Joseph.

Xander and Mitts stayed hidden, however, since Joseph still had not revealed himself to his brothers.

The brothers bought food to take back to Canaan. They loaded it in their food sacks and began to journey home.

There was one thing they didn't know, however. Joseph had ordered his servants to secretly place his silver cup in

Benjamin's food sack.

During the brothers' trip home, Joseph sent guards to catch up with them. They told the brothers that Joseph's cup had been stolen. They searched the food sacks and found the "stolen" cup in Benjamin's bag.

The brothers were frightened and confused. They were forced to return to Egypt to face Joseph.

"Please!" Judah begged Joseph. "We are innocent men! We stole nothing! Even if you don't believe us, please let Benjamin go. My brothers and I will stay here in prison. But Benjamin must return to our father!"

"No!" Joseph shouted. "Benjamin must remain here! The rest of you can go home to your father."

Hiding behind a pillar, Xander was still puzzled. "Why is Joseph acting this way?" he wondered. "I need to know the answer now!"

Chapter 9

Telling the Truth

Xander would have to wait for the eleven brothers to leave, so he could come out of hiding and ask Joseph to explain his actions.

Instead, Judah made one final appeal to Joseph.

"Please let our youngest brother go," he begged, nearly crying. "Our father loves him so very dearly. If he sees us return home without Benjamin, I'm afraid it will kill him."

Then Judah added, "I promised our father that Benjamin would be safe with me. If that promise is broken, I will bear the terrible blame forever and ever."

Xander peeked from behind the pillar to see what Joseph would do. He saw that Joseph was moved to tears by Judah's appeal.

At last, Joseph could no longer hide the truth from his brothers.

"I am Joseph!" he cried. "Is my father really still alive?"

The eleven brothers were speechless. They couldn't believe it was their brother Joseph who stood before them.

The brothers felt both fear and shame. They feared what Joseph might

now do to them. And they felt ashamed for selling him as a slave so long ago.

Yet Joseph spoke kindly to his brothers. "Don't feel sad that you sold me," he said. "It was all part of God's plan, so our family would survive during these years of hunger."

Joseph hugged his brothers, and they all cried together.

Then Joseph said, "Return home and tell Father to come here to Egypt with everyone in our family and all their belongings. All of you can live in the land of Goshen. I'll make sure that you have enough food, and fields to raise sheep."

The eleven brothers left Egypt and returned home to Canaan.

Meanwhile, Xander ran to Joseph. "Please tell me now, Joseph," he begged. "Why did you wait so long to let your brothers know who you really were?"

Joseph put his arm on Xander's shoulder and smiled.

"When my brothers first came to Egypt," he explained, "Benjamin was not with them. I remembered my first dream of long ago, where eleven bundles of grain were bowing down to mine. I had to get Benjamin to come to Egypt, so the dream would come true. When all eleven brothers bowed to me, the dream was fulfilled."

"Wow!" Xander gasped. "I'd completely forgotten about that dream!" Joseph continued, "Yes, but more importantly, I had to see if their hatred for me when I was my father's favorite had moved to Benjamin now that he is the favorite. I had to know if they changed their ways and regretted selling me. I had to know if they would protect Benjamin or leave him to be put in prison in Egypt!"

"That's wonderful!" Xander cried. "Soon your entire family will be together again, after all these years."

"Yes," Joseph agreed. "With God's help, dreams really can come true."

Suddenly, Xander looked sad.

"What's wrong?" Joseph asked.

Xander petted Mitts as he spoke. "All this talk of family reminds me that I've also been away from my own family for a long time," Xander said softly.

"Would you like to go back to them?" Joseph asked.

"Oh, yes!" Xander cried. "And I wouldn't complain anymore about having to wear Kevin's hand-me-downs, either. Now I see the harm that can come from jealousy and sibling rivalry."

"I know, I know," Joseph said,

laughing. "I learned the hard way, too."

Then Joseph added, "I have an idea. After my family arrives here, I think I know a way you can return home."

Xander's eyes opened wide. "Really?" he gasped. "That would be wonderful!"

Soon the big day came. Jacob arrived in Egypt with his entire family -- seventy members in all! Out of respect for his position in Egypt, they all bowed to Joseph, fulfilling his second dream.

Xander watched as Joseph hugged and kissed the members of his family. It made Xander miss his own family even more.

Finally, Joseph came over to Xander. He held a large sack.

"What's in the bag?" Xander asked.

Joseph smiled as he reached inside.

Xander couldn't believe what he pulled out--the coat of many colors! It had been washed, and now shone brightly once again.

Joseph put on the coat. He turned to Xander and said, "Look behind you, my friend. Tell me what you see."

Xander turned around slowly. He could hardly believe it! There in the sky was a rainbow! It looked exactly like the one that Xander had ridden many years before. As before, one end of the rainbow connected to the colors of the coat.

"Xander, this is your way home," Joseph said, smiling. "You can return the same way you got here. Just ride the rainbow!"

Xander was filled with both joy and sadness. He hugged Joseph tightly. Xander had been with Joseph for a long time. He was like another brother to Xander, and Xander was going to miss him.

Joseph said, "Thank you for being with me all this time. You made this ordeal and adventure much easier."

Xander's eyes started to well up. "Thank you for creating this rainbow," Xander said.

Joseph wagged a finger and said, "Xander, I did not create this rainbow. God did. Remember, it is God who answers all our prayers."

"Of course," Xander said. "I'll remember that."

Xander checked that he had all his belongings. He buckled his explorer's belt tightly. He made sure his brown fedora hat sat snugly on his head.

Finally, Xander picked up Mitts and held him close.

"Come on, pal, we've got a wild ride ahead of us," he said.

Xander waved goodbye to Joseph as he climbed onto the foot of the rainbow. He gently placed Mitts in front of him. Then the two of them began to crawl slowly up the arc.

Chapter 10

Oh, Brother!

Xander moved carefully along the rainbow, with Mitts just in front of him. Xander managed to keep his balance as he crawled along the arc.

The two were halfway to the top of the rainbow. Suddenly, a strange magnetic force began to pull them. Xander remembered that the same thing had happened when they climbed the rainbow the first time.

Xander and Mitts were no longer crawling. Now, they were sliding up the rainbow -- without even trying!

When they reached the top of the arc, Xander looked down.

"Look, Mitts!" Xander called. "We're above the clouds once again!"

Xander knew what was coming next. Quickly, he grabbed Mitts and placed him on his lap.

"Hold on, Mitts!" he cried. "We're about to slide down the rainbow!"

Sure enough, Xander and Mitts began to zoom down the arc. Bright colors blurred in front of their eyes. Red! Orange! Yellow! Green! Blue! Purple!

Finally, they reached the ground. They were back in the park -- in the same spot where they had left many years earlier.

"What a trip!" Xander cried. "I can't

wait till we get home!"

Xander and Mitts ran for home without stopping. Soon they were in front of their house.

The two raced through the front door. Xander was sweating from the long run.

"Mom! Dad! I'm home!" he cried.

His parents walked into the room. Xander immediately ran to them hugging them tightly. He felt like he had not seen them in a very long time.

"Do you know who I am?" Xander asked nervously.

Mom and Dad laughed.

"Of course we know who you are, Alexander," Dad chuckled. "Although you're sweating more than usual."

"That's because Mitts and I just ran

all the way from the park," Xander explained.

"Is everything okay, Alexander?" Mom asked. "We didn't think you'd be back so soon."

"Back so soon?" Xander exclaimed. "But I've been gone for years!"

"Years?" Dad laughed. "I know they say 'time flies,' but I don't think it flies *that* fast!"

"No, really!" Xander insisted. "Mitts and I rode a rainbow all the way back to the days of the Bible. We met Joseph and his brothers!"

Mom felt Xander's forehead. "I think all that running has left you a little dizzy dear," she said. "Maybe you should go to your room and lie down for a while."

"No, seriously, Mom," Xander insisted.

"Joseph and I were sold as slaves in Egypt, and then we helped feed the people there, and then I rode the rainbow back home."

Dad smiled and patted his son's head. "Of course, Alexander, whatever you say," he said.

Xander was frustrated that his parents didn't believe him, and he plopped on to the sofa. Suddenly, Xander heard a clink in his pocket. Reaching in he pulled out a small silver cup. Joseph had a way of slipping these where you least expected it.

Xander was excited to be able to prove to his parents about his adventure. He was about to open his mouth, and then thought better of it. He slipped the small cup back into his pocket. "I think I will keep this to myself for now," he thought.

Just then, Kevin walked in. He was wearing the new sweater he had been

given that morning.

"Hey, Bro," Kevin said. "Are you still mad at me?"

Xander went over to Kevin and hugged him. "I'm not mad at all," Xander said, smiling. "I think you look great in that sweater."

"Really?" Kevin replied, surprised. "Because just a while ago, you seemed pretty jealous about the whole thing."

Xander thought about Joseph and his jealous brothers. He remembered how their sibling rivalry had almost led to deadly results.

"Kevin, I'm not jealous anymore," Xander said. "I promise I'll never be jealous of you again."

Just then, Dad snapped his fingers. "That reminds me!" he said. "Wait here one second."

Dad went into the next room and returned with a box. He handed it to Xander.

"Here, this is for you, Alexander," Dad said.

Xander was excited. He opened the box. Inside was a beautiful colored sweater. It looked exactly like the one Kevin wore.

"It's beautiful!" Xander cried, hugging Mom and Dad. "Thank you so much for the colorful gift."

"I hope you know that Mom and I love you and Kevin just the same," Dad said.

"I know," Xander nodded, smiling.

He put on his new sweater and stood next to Kevin.

"Now we look like twins!" Xander

said.

"Just remember that you're my *younger* brother," Kevin teased. "And if you ever cause me any more trouble, I'll have to make you my slave!"

Xander laughed. "Been there, done that!" he joked.

Only he wasn't kidding!

Dr. Hunter Talen, is a fictional character that was born in either 1947 or 1625. He was raised by his globetrotting archaeologist father, G. Therer Talen, and his mother Katherine "Kat" Klause-Talen, who had been a singer in silent films. He was exposed to many of the great archaeological sites across 5 continents before the age of ten. He attended *Der Spelunken Academy* in Gestalt and studied under the world renowned explorer Dr. Heverford "Ever" Last, graduating with his PhD at 17. By 20 he had already done extensive work translating the runes of the Upper Tribes of Invisiline and published his findings on the secret rituals of the Gurl Skowtz in three best selling volumes, all to international acclaim.

Talen inspired countless field archaeologists with his works, and has been awarded a *Pica Star* by the Adventuring Fellowship out of Genova. He has earned three "Bom Diggity" awards and is a member of the exclusive Secret Adventurers Club and of the surprisingly less exclusive Top Secret Adventurers Club. He currently calls the outer rim of the Mauna Lisa volcano home and base of operations in between expeditions.

Neil Kleid, the Xeric-Award winning cartoonist, authored *Ninety Candles*, *Brownsville*, and *The Big Kahn*. Neil has written for Marvel, DC, Dark Horse and Image Comics, Shadowline, NBM Publishing, Archaia Studios, Slave Labor Graphics, Random House and Puffin Graphics. He lives in New Jersey with his wife and kids, working on three graphic novels, several comic books, a novel and no sleep. Pray for him at www.rantcomics.com

Creation By Design's mission is to create educational and entertaining Biblical products that help children connect with God's word in an exciting, fun way. Using the latest in computer digital graphics, Creation By Design offers our children the images they are interested in and want to see, and offers parents a new way for our next generation to bond with Scripture. Come see what is new at www.creationbydesign.com

XANDER NASH:
HAS AN ADVENTURE JUST FOR YOU!

ISBN: 978-0-9828077-4-3

Also from

CREATION BY DESIGN™

Activity Books

Joseph & His Brothers
Artifacts of the Tabernacle
Creation of the World
The Ten Commandments

My Bible Cards™
Bible Trading Cards

Old Testament: Series A
Old Testament: Series B
New Testament: Series A

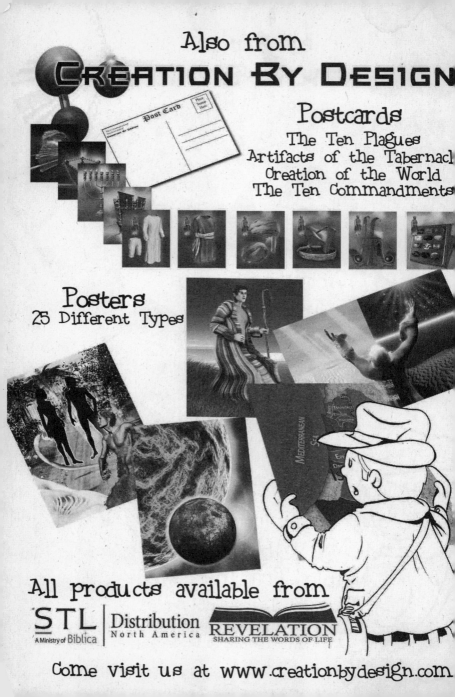

Also from
CREATION BY DESIGN

Postcards
The Ten Plagues
Artifacts of the Tabernacle
Creation of the World
The Ten Commandments

Posters
25 Different Types

All products available from

STL
A Ministry of Biblica

Distribution
North America

REVELATION
SHARING THE WORDS OF LIFE

Come visit us at www.creationbydesign.com